For my children
for ever,
no matter what.

BLOOMSBURY CHILDREN'S BOOKS
Bloomsbury Publishing Plc
50 Bedford Square, London WC1B 3DP, UK
29 Earlsfort Terrace, Dublin 2, Ireland

BLOOMSBURY, BLOOMSBURY CHILDREN'S BOOKS and the Diana logo
are trademarks of Bloomsbury Publishing Plc

First published in Great Britain in 1999 by Bloomsbury Publishing PLC

This paperback edition first published in 2014

A CIP catalogue record of this book is available from the British Library

ISBN 978 1 4088 5000 8
ISBN 978 1 4088 3905 8 (eBook)

12

Printed in China by C&C Offset Printing Co Ltd, Shenzhen, Guangdong

To find out more about our authors and books visit www.bloomsbury.com and sign up for our newsletters

No Matter What

BLOOMSBURY
CHILDREN'S BOOKS
LONDON   OXFORD   NEW YORK   NEW DELHI   SYDNEY

Small was feeling
grim and dark.

Playing toss and fling and squash,
yell and scream and bang and crash.
Break and snap and bash and batter . . .

"Good grief," said Large.
"What *is* the matter?"

Small said,
"I'm a grim and grumpy
little Small
and nobody
loves me at all."

"Oh Small," said Large. "Grumpy or not,
I'll always love you no matter what."

Small said, "If I was a grizzly bear,
would you still love me,
would you care?"

"Of course," said Large,
"bear or not,
I'll always love you
no matter what."

Small said, "But if I turned into a bug,

would you still love me and give me a hug?"

"Of course," said Large,
"bug or not,

I'll always love you
no matter what."

"No matter what?" said Small
and smiled.

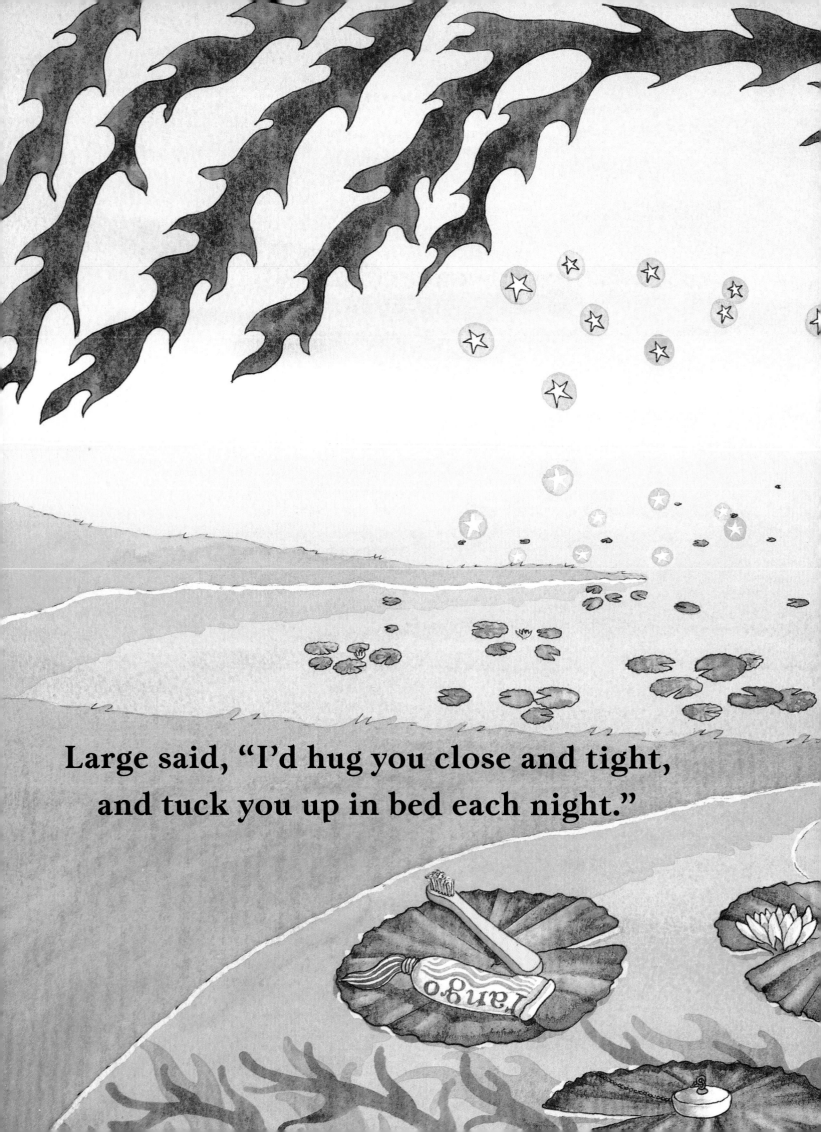

Large said, "I'd hug you close and tight,
and tuck you up in bed each night."

"Does love wear out," said Small,
"does it break or bend?
Can you fix it, stick it,
does it mend?"

"Oh help," said Large, "I'm not that clever,
I just know I'll love you for ever."

Small said, "But what about when we're dead and gone, would you love me then, does love go on?"

Large held Small snug
as they looked out at the night,
at the moon in the dark
and the stars shining bright.
"Small, look at the stars –
how they shine and glow,
but some of those stars died
a long time ago."

"Still they shine in the evening skies
love, like starlight, never dies."